# Little Bird Lost

For Hugo – PH

STRIPES PUBLISHING LTD
An imprint of the Little Tiger Group
1 Coda Studios, 189 Munster Road, London SW6 6AW

First published in Great Britain in 2020

Text copyright © Patricia Hegarty, 2020
Illustrations © Sebastiaan Van Doninck, 2020

ISBN: 978-1-78895-117-3

A CIP catalogue record for this book is available from the British Library.

Printed and bound in China.

STP/1800/0265/0419

2 4 6 8 10 9 7 5 3 1

# Little Bird Lost

Patricia Hegarty

Illustrated by

## Sebastiaan Van Doninck

STRIPES

Our story begins on a summer breeze,
    Whispering gently through the trees...

Summer

"*Chick-kee! Chick-kee!*"

The sound was so faint that Deer almost missed it. But there it was again.

"*Chick-kee! Chick-kee!*"

Deer paused and looked around.
"Hello? Is someone there?"

"I'm here!"
came a tiny voice.

Deer looked down and
saw a small yellow bird
among some twigs and
leaves on the ground.

"Careful, somebody might
tread on you down there."

"That's what I'm afraid of!"
cheeped the bird.

Deer noticed then that one of the bird's
wings was sticking out at an odd angle.

"Are you hurt?" enquired Deer.

"Yes, and I can't fly," said the bird plaintively.

Deer leaned forward until his antlers
were almost touching the ground.

"Hop aboard, Little Bird.
You'll be safe with me."

"This is very kind of you, Deer.
Thank you for helping me."

Little Bird jumped up but then...

## "Oof!"

He slid back down again.

"Oops! Let's try it a bit more slowly this time..."

Deer took careful steps through the wood with
Little Bird perched perilously atop his antlers.

"One minute I was flying happily through the sky
with my flock, the next minute – crash, bang,
wallop! I was on my bottom on the forest floor!"

"You must have hit a branch, Little Bird."

"But how will I find the rest of my flock now?"
Little Bird thought he might cry.

"Don't worry, Little Bird," said Deer gently. "I have
lots of friends in the forest – we will help you."

Just then the pair heard a distant honking
sound. They looked up to the sky to see
a flock of geese flying overhead.

"Look, Deer!" cried Little Bird,
flapping his good wing excitedly.

"Those birds are much bigger than my flock, but maybe they are flying to the same place!"

"Quick, let's ask them! Chick-kee, Geese!" Little Bird called out as loudly as he could, but the geese were too far away to hear.

When they reached the clearing, Little Bird told everyone how he had ended up on the forest floor.

"But surely you know where you were flying to?" Squirrel interrupted.

"No. You see, I've never made the flight before – it was my first time," replied Little Bird.

"What's the matter with your wing?" asked kindly Rabbit.

"I hurt it when I fell," said Little Bird.

"It looks to me as if it's broken.
It will take time to heal," said Fox.

"Yes, it looks broken!"
squeaked the field mice.

Then Big Old Bear spoke. "I don't know exactly where your flock were going, but I'd guess they were heading somewhere warmer."

"Yes, yes, that sounds right!" chirped Little Bird.

"So, Little Bird, you need to follow the sun."

"Yes, follow the sun!" chorused the field mice. "Big Old Bear always knows best!"

"But how can he possibly follow the sun if he can't fly?" demanded Porcupine crossly.

Little Bird looked crestfallen.

"Don't mind him," said Deer. "He's always a bit prickly. Why don't I go with you and help you?"

"Yes, yes!" sang the field mice. "Deer is clever – he'll know where to go."

All the forest creatures
turned out to wave farewell
to Deer and Little Bird as
they set off on their journey.

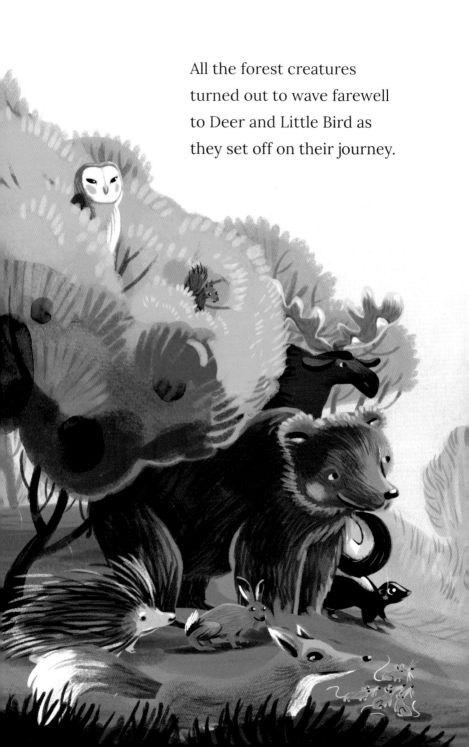

"Good luck, Little Bird!" said Rabbit.

"Goodbye!" called Squirrel.

"Don't forget us!" cried Big Old Bear.

"No, don't forget us!" sang the field mice.

"It's a crazy plan..." grumbled Porcupine.

But Deer and Little Bird were already on their way.

"Do you want a lift, Little Bird?" asked Deer.

"No thank you, Deer, I will hop for a while –
there are so many interesting things to
see on the ground!"

Deer strode off, with Little Bird
hopping along behind him.

Little Bird was so excited that their
journey was constantly interrupted
by each new discovery.

"Chick-kee, look at me!" called Little Bird,
peeking out from a tree stump.

Deer smiled. "Come on, Little Bird,
we'd better keep going."

*Autumn leaves fall to the ground,*
*A blaze of colour all around...*

Autumn

"Do you think we're nearly there yet, Deer?"

Little Bird was hopping among the leaves that were whirling and twirling through the air.

"I don't think so, Little Bird. We haven't been going very long, but I'm sure we are getting there."

"Yippee!" chirruped Little Bird.

Deer turned around but his companion
was nowhere to be found.

"Little Bird?" he called.

"*Chick-kee!* Surprise! Here I am!"
laughed Little Bird, as he popped up
from a pile of leaves.

Deer shook his head and smiled.
"Somebody's feeling better!"

The pair kept walking all day, until the sun began to set.

"It's funny," observed Little Bird. "We've been walking a very long time, but the sun never seems to get any nearer, does it?"

"I think we just need to keep going, Little Bird."

"I've made up a little song to pass the time!" Little Bird chirped.

Chick-kee, chick-kee!
Deer and me,
Having fun,
Following the sun.
Chick-kee, chick-kee,
Deer and me!

The pair chose a nice sheltered spot to settle
down for the night.

"Goodnight, Deer."

"Goodnight, Little Bird."

"Deer?"

"Yes, Little Bird?"

"I don't like the dark..."

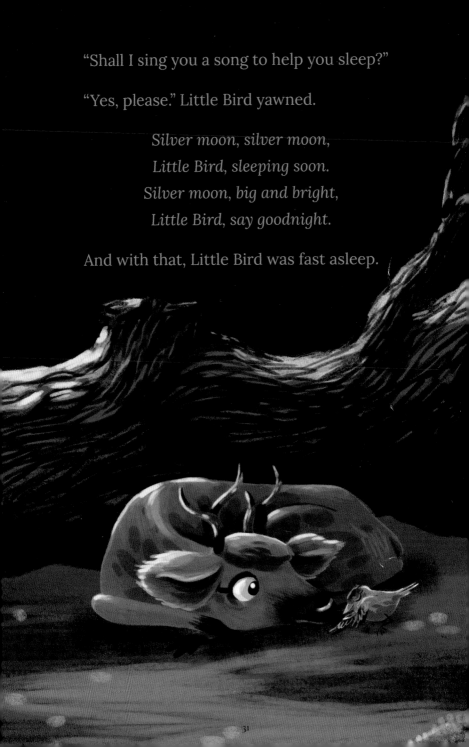

"Shall I sing you a song to help you sleep?"

"Yes, please." Little Bird yawned.

> *Silver moon, silver moon,*
> *Little Bird, sleeping soon.*
> *Silver moon, big and bright,*
> *Little Bird, say goodnight.*

And with that, Little Bird was fast asleep.

Deer was awoken by a tiny cheeping
sound right by his ear.

"Deer, wake up! I can hear a funny noise."

"Don't worry, Little Bird, there are lots of
funny noises in the woods at night," said Deer.

He closed his eyes again but then...

"*Chick-kee!* Help! Help!" cried Little Bird.

Deer was on his feet in a flash. To his horror,
he saw that Little Bird was pinned up against
the tree trunk by a large, hungry-looking wolf.

Deer rushed at the wolf and prodded
him as hard as he could with his antlers.
The wolf leaped back in shock and Deer
seized the opportunity.

Little Bird clung on to Deer's antlers
and they raced through the woods,
with the snarling wolf hot on their heels.

"I'm going as fast as I can,"

panted Deer.

Suddenly the pair emerged from the trees to find themselves on the bank of a wide, fast-flowing river.

"What now?" exclaimed Little Bird, looking behind him to see the wolf closing on them.

"Hold on tight, Little Bird – we're going in!" shouted Deer.

And with that, Deer began to wade into the water...

Soon Deer was up to his neck in the swirling water, with Little Bird perched as high up on his antlers as he could go.

"The wolf is swimming after us!" cried Little Bird.

The pair were now in the middle of the river,
where the current was strongest.

"Keep going, Deer, I think he's giving up,"
squeaked Little Bird.

And sure enough, as Deer swam closer to the opposite bank, the wolf began to disappear into the distance, swept downstream by the river's current.

"*Chick-kee!* That was a close shave!"
sang Little Bird.

"It certainly was," replied Deer.
"I'm exhausted. Let's find somewhere
to settle down and get some sleep."

Deer and Little Bird found a sheltered
spot in which to rest.

"If you like, I could sing you one of my songs, Deer," chirruped Little Bird.

"Deer?"

But Deer was fast asleep.

The air is chill, icy winds blow,
Earth rests beneath a blanket of snow...

# Winter

Deer and Little Bird continued on their journey,
leaving the forest behind them and climbing
across rocks and scrubland.
The harsh landscape was beginning to slow
them down and the weather was getting colder.

One morning, Little Bird awoke to find
that the whole world had turned white!

"*Chick-kee, chick-kee!*" he chirped
in delight, as he hopped about, making
pretty patterns with his feet.

Suddenly Little Bird had an idea...

"Wake up, Deer, I've got
something to show you! Look!"

"That's wonderful, Little Bird, thank you.
You are a very special friend."
Deer smiled.

Deer and Little Bird spent the morning playing in the snow, before setting off on their journey once again.

"Brrrrr, I'm cold," shivered Little Bird.

"I know," replied Deer.

"And I'm really tired."

"I know, Little Bird."

"And I'm really, really hungry..."

It was beginning to get dark and once again
the pair were looking for shelter.

"How about here?" suggested Little Bird,
pointing to a hollow log.

"I don't think I can squeeze in there,
Little Bird!" laughed Deer.

"What about this?" called Little Bird,
pointing to a wide branch.

"How would we get up there?"

"Good point, Deer... Ah, I know!"

Little Bird pointed to a rabbit burrow.

Deer shook his head.
"We'd better keep looking, Little Bird."

"Little Bird?"

Little Bird was nowhere to be seen.

Deer called out again, but there was no reply.

"Are you hiding? Come out now..."

As the sky darkened the snow began
to fall more and more heavily.

"Little Bird, if you're playing a joke, it's not funny any more," called Deer through the blizzard.

But there was no reply.

Then all of a sudden, Little Bird hopped
up as if from nowhere.

"*Chick-kee!* Have I got a treat for you, Deer!"

Deer was so happy to find his friend safe and sound
that it took him a moment to notice the ants' nest.

"Hmmm, I think I'll stick to my
acorns, thanks," muttered Deer.

Little Bird popped some ants in his mouth and
chirped happily, all thoughts of shelter forgotten.

But the snow was coming down harder than ever.

"Look over here, Little Bird," called Deer, "I think I've found somewhere for us to shelter for the night."

Little Bird looked doubtfully into the gloom of the cave and shuddered. "It's very dark, isn't it?"

"I know," said Deer gently. "Don't worry,
we'll stay close together."

The pair inched slowly into the cave and
found a dry spot in which to settle.

"Deer, will you sing me a song?" pleaded Little Bird.

*Little Bird, in a cave,*
*Little Bird, oh so brave—*

"What's that flapping noise?
Maybe my flock are here!"

Little Bird hopped about excitedly.

Deer listened. There was indeed a
flapping noise in the cave, and a sort of squeaking
sound. "I'm afraid that's not your flock, Little Bird.
Now don't panic, they're ... bats."

"Chick-kee! I'm scared of bats... Erm, what are bats?"

Deer reassured Little Bird that the bats
wouldn't bother them – in fact, they would use
their special radar to avoid them.

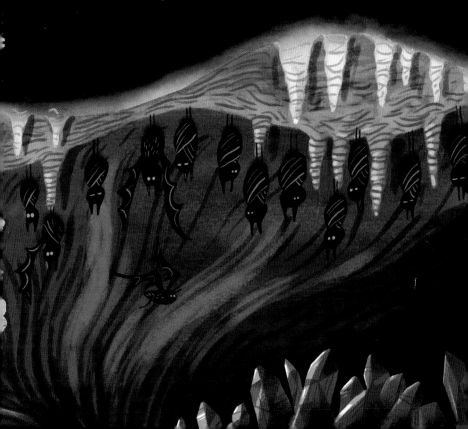

Deer and Little Bird huddled together in the cave, but it wasn't easy to sleep. When they'd run out of songs, Deer suggested a story.

"Once upon a time," he began, "there was a very brave little bird who set off on an epic journey..."

"I hope this story has a happy ending," cheeped Little Bird.

As Deer continued his story, the cave began to glow with tiny pricks of light, getting brighter and brighter.

"Fireflies!" exclaimed Deer.

By the light of the fireflies, their overnight shelter
was transformed into a magical home filled
with sparkling stalagmites and stalactites,
and colourful rocks.

"...and they all lived happily ever after,"
whispered Deer.

But guess what?
Little Bird was already
fast asleep.

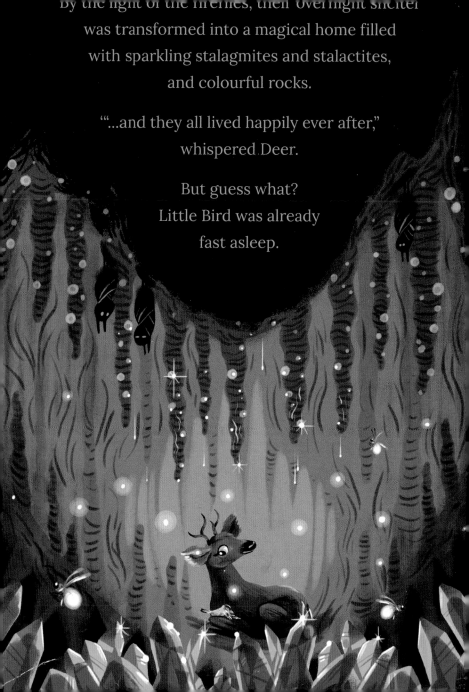

The last of the snow has melted away,
The sun is rising on a clear blue day...

Spring

In the bright sunlight, green
shoots and buds were appearing
everywhere.

Deer and Little Bird felt full of fresh
hope as they made their way across
the fields and meadows.

One morning, Little Bird woke early
and watched in wonder at all the
activity going on around him.

He was especially fascinated by
the birds busily collecting twigs
and leaves for their nests. It gave
him an idea...

"*Ta-da*! I've built a nest, Deer!"
chirruped Little Bird proudly.

"That's very clever of you, Little Bird,"
laughed Deer, "but I don't think it will last
very long when I start to move..."

"Never mind, Deer! Nothing can spoil
my mood on this beautiful bright morning.
It's so sunny all the time – and that means we
must be getting closer to finding my flock now."

"I think you're right, Little Bird.
Come on, let's keep going."

Eventually they stopped for a short rest.
As Little Bird hopped about happily,
Deer spotted someone watching them.

"Hello, I'm Deer," he said.

"And I'm Doe. It's nice to meet you! I've been
watching you and your little friend."

Deer told Doe all about their journey
to find Little Bird's flock.

"It sounds like a real adventure," said Doe.

"You can say that again!" laughed Deer.

"Deer, I think it's time to go now,"
called Little Bird.

"Just a minute, Little Bird," replied Deer.

He turned back to Doe and continued
talking to her.

A few minutes passed before Little Bird tried again.

"Come on Deer, it'll be getting dark soon!"

The afternoon wore on and Deer
seemed in no hurry to move.

So Little Bird began to play a game, hopping
on and off a rock and flapping his wings.

He realized it had been a long time since
his wing felt painful.

After a while, Little Bird hopped up onto
a bigger rock and tried jumping from that
instead, flapping furiously.

He'd almost forgotten how to use his wings.

Then Little Bird noticed something
out of the corner of his eye.

Slinking silently towards Deer and Doe
was a mean-looking cougar!

"Look out!" called Little Bird, as loudly
as he could. But Deer and Doe didn't hear him.
Little Bird felt a surge of panic ...
then did what came naturally to him.

"*Chick-kee! Chick-kee!*" exclaimed
Little Bird as he swooped through the air,
flapping his wings wildly to warn his friends.

He looked down to see the cougar
disappearing into the trees.

"Look at me, I'm *flying!*"
tweeted Little Bird joyfully.

Little Bird flew loop-the-loops around
Deer and Doe as he chirruped excitedly.

"It's wonderful that you can fly again,"
said Deer.

"What's that noise?" asked Doe,
as she peered up at the sky.

Little Bird and Deer
looked up to see...

"It's my flock!" cried Little Bird.

With that he flapped his wings and
flew up to join the other birds.

Deer and Doe looked up to see
Little Bird fading into the distance.

"Well, I suppose I should feel happy,"
murmured Deer. "But I'm going to
miss my little friend..."

"*Chick-kee!* You didn't think I'd leave without saying goodbye, did you?" said Little Bird, flapping down to Deer.

"I don't know what I would have done without you," cheeped Little Bird. "How can I ever thank you?"

"There's no need to thank me. I've had adventures I could never have imagined and made a wonderful new friend..."

Doe nudged him gently.

"Two wonderful new friends!" laughed Deer.

"I will never forget you," continued Little Bird,
"and I can drop in to see you when I'm flying
past with my flock."

"Just be careful you don't hit any branches!"
laughed Deer.

With that, Little Bird rose up into the sky.

"Goodbye, Little Bird, fly safely," called Deer.

"*Chick-kee, chick-kee!*" came the reply,
floating on the breeze.

*The End*